Dear Parents:

Congratulations! Your child is taking the first steps on an exciting journey. The destination? Independent reading!

STEP INTO READING® will help your child get there. The program offers five steps to reading success. Each step includes fun stories and colorful art or photographs. In addition to original fiction and books with favorite characters, there are Step into Reading Non-Fiction Readers, Phonics Readers and Boxed Sets, Sticker Readers, and Comic Readers—a complete literacy program with something to interest every child.

Learning to Read, Step by Step!

Ready to Read   Preschool–Kindergarten
• big type and easy words • rhyme and rhythm • picture clues
For children who know the alphabet and are eager to begin reading.

Reading with Help   Preschool–Grade 1
• basic vocabulary • short sentences • simple stories
For children who recognize familiar words and sound out new words with help.

Reading on Your Own   Grades 1–3
• engaging characters • easy-to-follow plots • popular topics
For children who are ready to read on their own.

Reading Paragraphs   Grades 2–3
• challenging vocabulary • short paragraphs • exciting stories
For newly independent readers who read simple sentences with confidence.

Ready for Chapters   Grades 2–4
• chapters • longer paragraphs • full-color art
For children who want to take the plunge into chapter books but still like colorful pictures.

STEP INTO READING® is designed to give every child a successful reading experience. The grade levels are only guides; children will progress through the steps at their own speed, developing confidence in their reading.

Remember, a lifetime love of reading starts with a single step!

P9-DEM-865

All rights reserved. Published in the United States by Random House Children's Books, a division of Penguin Random House LLC, 1745 Broadway, New York, NY 10019, and in Canada by Penguin Random House Canada Limited, Toronto.

Step into Reading, Random House, and the Random House colophon are registered trademarks of Penguin Random House LLC.

Visit us on the Web!
StepIntoReading.com
rhcbooks.com

Educators and librarians, for a variety of teaching tools, visit us at RHTeachersLibrarians.com

ISBN 978-0-593-38233-2 (trade) — ISBN 978-0-593-38234-9 (lib. bdg.)
ISBN 978-0-593-338235-6 (ebook)

Printed in the United States of America

10 9 8 7 6 5 4 3 2 1

SPACE JAM
A NEW LEGACY

JOIN THE TEAM!

by Tex Huntley

illustrated by Red Central Ltd

Random House 🏠 New York

LeBron James is a
great basketball player.

He loves to play!

LeBron needs a team.
Who will join?

Bugs Bunny is ready to play!

Marvin
the Martian
has a spaceship.
LeBron and Bugs
will use it to find
more players!

They visit Gotham City.
They need
basketball players,
not Super Heroes!

"Hey!" asks LeBron.

"Who is the sidekick?"

Daffy Duck is
the Tune Squad's coach.
He has team spirit!

Lola is the best
Tune on the team!

Speedy Gonzales is small,
but no one can catch him!

You cannot keep
Tweety down!

Gossamer and
Foghorn Leghorn are
big and strong.

They are unstoppable!

Wile E. Coyote and the Road Runner are finally on the same team!

Watch out for Taz.

He is wild
on the court!

Elmer Fudd,

Porky Pig,

and Yosemite Sam
never give up!

Granny,

Sylvester,

and Penelope

complete the team!

This is one all-star squad!

The Tune Squad
is ready for anything.
Go, team!